W9-BBQ-344

　　有一隻老猴子在街上買了
兩隻杯子、兩個碗、兩把茶
壺和兩隻盤子，準備回家。
　　牠用右手拿起兩隻杯子，
左手提起兩把茶壺，可是，
地上卻還有盤子和碗。牠又
用左手拿起兩個碗，右手提
起兩隻盤子，可是地上還有
杯子和茶壺。牠放下又拿起
來，拿起來又放下，試了十
幾次，牠開始著急了。

這時，有個人從前面走過來，手裡提著籃子，籃裡裝著五隻盤子、五個碗、五個茶壺，和五個杯子。老猴子看了很高興，大叫：「哇！籃子可以裝那麼多東西呀！」

老猴子也買了一個籃子，把杯碗盤壺全放了進去。這以後，老猴子就一直記著：「籃子能裝很多東西。」

By this time, a man holding a basket passed by her. In the basket there were five plates, five bowls, five teapots, and five cups. Seeing this, the old monkey screamed with joy, "Wow! A basket surely can hold a lot of things!"

Then the old monkey bought a basket, and placed all the cups, bowls, plates, teapots into it. From then on, the old monkey kept in mind: "A basket can hold many things."

One day the monkey's house caught on fire. The old monkey quickly started to move her belongings. She told a smaller monkey to fill the basket with water. The small monkey left right away.

After a long time, it still hadn't returned. The fire became worse and worse.

一天，猴子家起了火，老猴子忙著搬東西，叫小猴子提籃子去打水。

小猴子去了半天，還不回來。火越燒越大了。

The old monkey was so worried that she ran to the river herself. The small monkey was still sweating by the river trying to get some water.

The old monkey screamed, "You rotten child! You are taking forever to get back. The house is almost burnt down..." Before the old monkey had finished talking, she grabbed the basket.

The small monkey was trembling as if he had been whipped. He said, "Mommy, I did get a whole basket of water, but as soon as I pick up the basket, the water disappears. That's why I have taken so long."

老猴子很著急，連忙去河邊看看。小猴子還趴在河邊打水，流了一身的汗。

老猴子大聲罵説：「該死的東西，半天不見回來，房子都快燒掉了…………」老猴子話沒説完，一把將籃子搶了過去。

小猴子像挨了揍一樣，發抖的説：「媽媽，我明明打滿了一籃子水，可是一提起來，就沒有了，這就是爲什麼我耽擱這麼久的原因。」

The old monkey answered angrily, "Stop fooling around. Not only can baskets hold things, they can hold lots of things! I have carried cups, bowls, plates, and teapots in this basket. You silly child! I'll prove it to you."

The old monkey bent down to get the water, but the same thing happened. She tried over and over again. Still she couldn't pick up even half a drop of water.

老猴子生氣的說：「胡說八道！籃子不但能裝東西，還能裝很多很多呢！我就裝過杯子、碗、盤和茶壺。你這個笨東西，我做給你看！」

老猴子彎下腰打起水來，可是，老猴子跟小猴子一樣，打了半天，都沒有打上半滴水來。

In the end, the house burnt down. Yet the old monkey still couldn't figure out why the basket wasn't useful anymore.

最後，房子給火燒光了，老猴子還想不通籃子爲什麼不管用了。

Parental Guide

Why wasn't the basket useful anymore? Leave this question for the children to answer.

There is an old saying, "Drawing water from a well with a basket is a waste of energy. Past experiences can be useful only if you think wisely." This is the theme of the story. Not only children make errors because of limited knowledge about a tool but also because they don't know how to use tools properly. Adults may even have these problems. The monkey's experiences are analogous to our own.

Lazy Wife & the Bread Ring

懶老婆吃圓餅

A long time ago, in a small town, there was a baker. Though he was very hard working, he had married a lazy wife.

How lazy was his wife? She didn't cook and didn't do the laundry. Every chore in the house was done by the baker himself. But he didn't become angry at all because he adored his wife. He was afraid that his wife would become tired out if she did anything.

從前，在一個小城裡，有一個燒餅師傅。他做事非常勤快，卻娶了一個懶惰的老婆。

這個懶老婆，怎麼懶呢？原來她不煮飯，也不洗衣服，家裡大大小小的事兒，全部都是燒餅師傅一個人做，但是，他一點兒都不生氣，因為他很疼老婆，怕老婆做事累壞了！

The lazy wife did nothing all day. She ate then slept, ate then slept. She became fatter and fatter. Gradually, she became so fat that she couldn't even get out of bed. Everyday the baker had to stand in front of her bed to give her food and water.

懶老婆整天不做事，吃飽了就睡，睡飽了又吃，吃吃睡睡，身體就變更越來越胖了。慢慢的，她已經胖得不能起床，所以，每天都是燒餅師傅在床前，餵她吃飯、喝水。

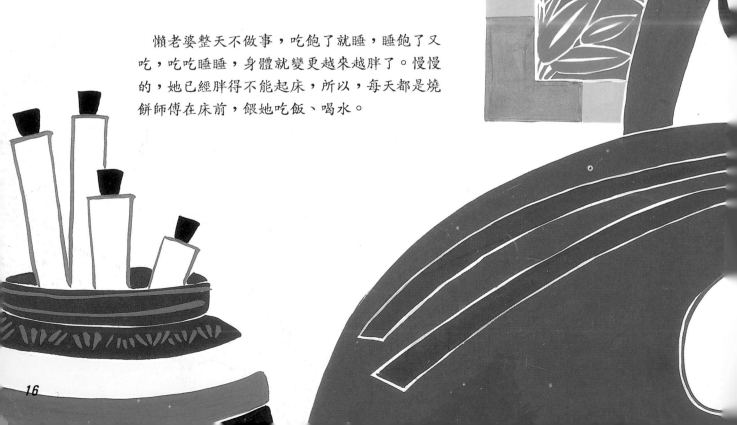

One day, the baker received a letter from his family. His mother had become sick because she missed him very much and wanted him to go back to the country to visit her.

After the baker read the letter, he became worried. He closed down his shop and was ready to head home.

有一天，燒餅師傅接到老家寫來的信，說他的媽媽想他想得生病了，要他趕快回鄉下去探望媽媽。

燒餅師傅看了信，急得不得了，把店門一關，就要回鄉下去。

他轉頭一想：「糟糕！我若回鄉下去，誰給老婆餵飯倒水，捶背洗腳呢？我還是不回去好了！」

可是，他又想到媽媽生病了，應該回去看看，不然放心不下。

「唉！怎麼辦呢？」他覺得回去也不對，不回去也不對，急得團團轉。

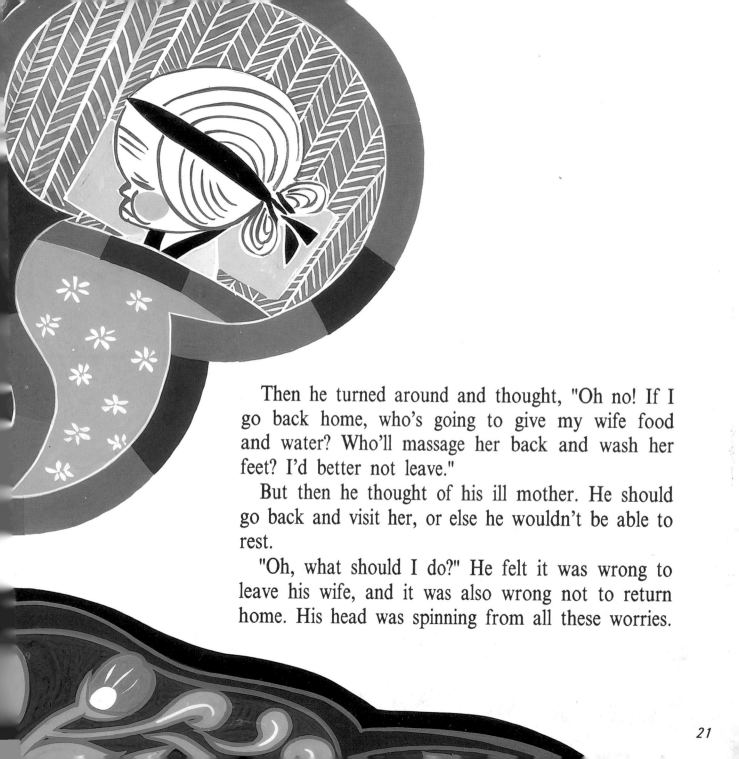

Then he turned around and thought, "Oh no! If I go back home, who's going to give my wife food and water? Who'll massage her back and wash her feet? I'd better not leave."

But then he thought of his ill mother. He should go back and visit her, or else he wouldn't be able to rest.

"Oh, what should I do?" He felt it was wrong to leave his wife, and it was also wrong not to return home. His head was spinning from all these worries.

「啊！有了！」燒餅師傅想到了一個好法子。他連夜做了一個十斤重的大圈餅，然後，把餅套在老婆的脖子上，說：「老婆，媽媽生病了，我得回家去看看。這圈餅夠你吃個十幾天，等你吃完，我也回來了！」

懶老婆只哼了一聲，連眼皮也懶得抬一下呢！燒餅師傅這才放心的回鄉下去了。

"Ah, that's it!" the baker thought of a grand idea. He stayed up all night to make a 10-pound ring of bread. Then he placed the ring around his wife's neck and said, "My dear, Mom is sick, I have to go home and care for her. This ring will last you more than 10 days. Before you're finished eating it, I should be back home."

The lazy wife replied with a grunt, not even bothering to lift up her eyelids. Then the baker got himself ready to return to his mother's home.

When the baker's mom saw that her son had come home, she immediately felt better. After a few more days, she had completely recovered.

After his mom became healthy, the baker was once again very happy. Yet, then he started to miss his wife in the city. So he hastily returned home.

燒餅師傅的媽媽看見兒子回來，病就好多了。再過幾天，病就全好了！

燒餅師傅看見媽媽身體好了，心裡很高興，但是他很掛念城裡的老婆，所以又急急忙忙趕回店裡去。

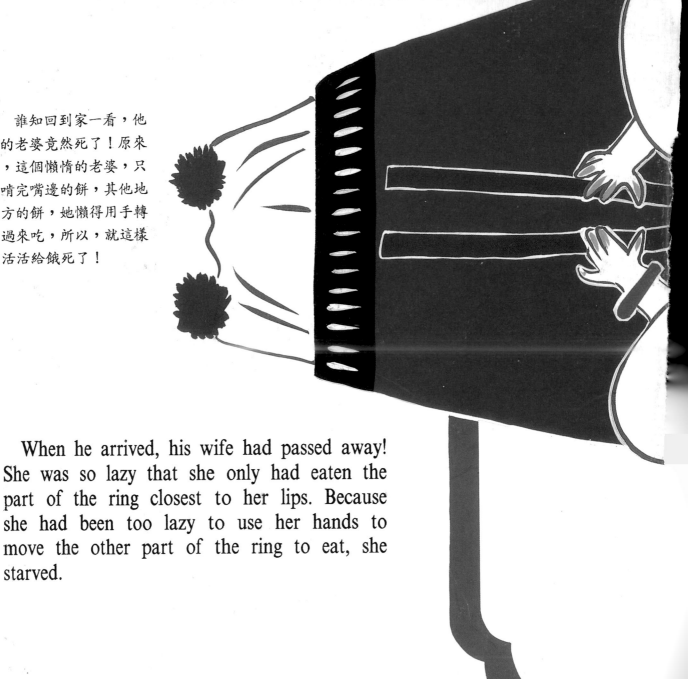

誰知回到家一看，他
的老婆竟然死了！原來
，這個懶惰的老婆，只
啃完嘴邊的餅，其他地
方的餅，她懶得用手轉
過來吃，所以，就這樣
活活給餓死了！

When he arrived, his wife had passed away!
She was so lazy that she only had eaten the
part of the ring closest to her lips. Because
she had been too lazy to use her hands to
move the other part of the ring to eat, she
starved.

"Lazy Wife and the Bread Ring" is a far-fetched fable used as a warning to children. Since children nowadays are usually well taken care of, they may not do any chores. They even may refuse to do chores. This story hints that lazy people will suffer in the end. After enjoying this story, hopefully children will value hard work and productivity.

Parental Guide